ELLA

written and illustrated by BILL PEET

HOUGHTON MIFFLIN COMPANY BOSTON

LIBRARY OF CONGRESS CATALOG CARD NUMBER: 63-20703
ISBN: 0-395-17577-1 REINFORCED EDITION
ISBN: 0-395-27269-6 SANDPIPER PAPERBACK EDITION
PRINTED IN THE U.S.A.

WOZ 20 19 18 17 16 15 14 13 12

Ella was such an intelligent creature
She had learned every trick that her trainer could teach her.
The crowds which packed in to the big top each night
Applauded and cheered Ella's act with delight.
She took it all in with her great ears outspread
So it all went directly to Ella's big head.
She grew as conceited and spoiled as could be
Which caused Ella trouble as you will soon see.

On one rainy day a big wagon got stuck
Up to its hubs in the mire and the muck.
A team of six horses had heaved for an hour
But the wheels wouldn't budge, for they needed more power.

So they called upon Ella, the elephant star,
The most powerful one in the circus by far.
With the least bit of effort, just one mighty butt,
She soon pushed the wagon right out of the rut.
Then drenched and bedraggled away Ella went
In a horrible temper on back to her tent.

"I'm a star," Ella grumbled, "How could they forget
And send me outside in the rain to get wet."
She was boiling with anger as everyone knew
So the elephant boss quickly called out his crew.
And with brushes and towels they scrubbed and they dried

Every square inch of her huge, wrinkled hide.
Then her robe was sent out to be dry-cleaned and pressed
And also they fluff-dried her ostrich-plume crest.
But all of this care didn't help Ella's mood
And day after day she continued to brood.

Early one morning they hauled the tents down
And packed up the circus to move out of town.
But Ella decided that she wouldn't go
"I'll teach them," she grumbled, "I'm quitting the show."

While the rest climbed aboard as they usually did,
She crouched down in back of a high fence and hid.
And the roustabouts had such struggle with Stella,
A bad-tempered zebra, they didn't see Ella!

But when the conductor gave one final shout
"All aboard!" And she saw the train start to pull out,
Ella stopped sulking as quick as a flash
And took off down the track in a wild frantic dash.

She ran on and on for mile after mile
Trumpeting through her long trunk all the while.
But she couldn't be heard for the clickety-clack
Of a hundred train wheels flying over the track.

"How silly," said Ella, "There's no need to hurry.
They'll stop when they reach the next town, so why worry.
It'll be a long walk, but I really don't care
Besides I could lose a few pounds here and there."
So she took her sweet time and enjoyed the fine scenery,
The rolling farm land trimmed in new summer greenery.

But the beautiful scenery stretched on and on
And before Ella knew it the morning was gone.
But she plodded ahead till the sun had gone down
Without even passing through one tiny town.
By then she was wearily dragging her feet
And was desperately wishing for something to eat.

So she wandered some distance away from the tracks
Till she came to a field full of fluffy haystacks
And she seized a long pitchfork with never a thought
That perhaps she'd be stealing and surely get caught.
And she'd leveled the haystack almost to the ground
When a farmer marched up with his scrawny old hound.

"I'll fix you!" he shouted, "for stealing my hay!"
As fiercely he jerked the sharp pitchfork away.
"Now get into the barn!" the old clodhopper cried,
"Before I just punch a few holes in your hide!"
Ella was never so frightened before
And she ran to the barn and squeezed through the door.
Then he slammed the door shut with a shattering jolt
And locked it up tight with a strong iron bolt.

"That old grouch," she grumbled, "can't treat me like that.
With one blow of my trunk I could knock him out flat.
Oh dear me! Now what am I saying," she sighed,
"If I harmed anyone why I'd be horrified.
But one thing for sure, I'm not going to stay.
The first thing tomorrow I'm running away."
Then resting her big, drowsy head on a beam
She was soon far away in an elephant dream.

Early next morning old Lucifer Kirk,
The grouchy old farmer, put Ella to work.
She was hitched to a plow and harnessed in chains
With Lucifer Kirk tightly gripping the reins.
And over one shoulder he carried a gun
In case she might try to break loose and run.
So escape seemed almost impossible now
Unless she could outwit the farmer somehow.

But he never let Ella get out of his sight
Until she was locked in the barn for the night.
And in a few days when the plowing was through
There was lots of weed pulling for Ella to do.
For a jungle of ragweed had grown to such height
That the vegetable garden was buried from sight.
And Ella had trouble right from the start
Telling the carrots and ragweed apart.
To remind her whenever she made a mistake,
Lucifer gave her a whack with a rake.

When every last weed had been taken away,
Ella picked apples the rest of the day.
She loved juicy apples, all elephants do.
As she filled up the baskets, she ate one or two.
But mean Mr. Kirk wouldn't stand for that trick
And each time she ate one he gave her a kick.
So Ella agreed after getting kicked twice
That a few tiny apples just weren't worth the price.

Once every week Ella mowed the front lawn
While Mr. Kirk sat on his porch looking on.
With the dog barking noisily close at her heels
She had trouble steering the lawn mower's wheels.

The poor dog had been lonely and sad all his life
On the farm with old Lucifer Kirk and his wife.
Now he'd become a much happier hound
With an elephant there to follow around.

When she gathered the eggs she could always expect
Her sensitive trunk to be badly hen-pecked,
For the instant she forced her huge head through the door
The hen house broke out in a violent uproar
As all the old hens madly tried to drive out
The egg-stealing monster with the long, snaky snout.

Watering flowers was a fun kind of work
So pleasant, in fact, she forgot Mr. Kirk.
And Ella recalled how she'd squealed with delight
When her friends brought her roses on opening night.
"I suppose," Ella thought, "being pampered so much
Might have spoiled me a bit—well, just a wee touch."

Feeding the pigs was by far the worst chore.
She had never detested anything more.
The smell of the swill, the loud squeals and grunts
Were entirely too much to take in all at once.
One day she decided too much was enough
And she went charging off in a horrible huff.

The hound was unhappy to see Ella go
So he started to bark and let Mr. Kirk know.
Alas for poor Ella, she hadn't gone far
When the farmer took off in his old touring car.
Then in desperation she pulled a fast trick
And blew up a dust cloud so dense and so thick
Mr. Kirk couldn't see and he cut down his speed
While Ella raced onward increasing her lead.

Then all of a sudden she ran out of luck.
She came to an old covered bridge and got stuck.
By the time she was able to squeeze her way out
The farmer arrived in his old runabout.
When he pointed his blunderbuss square in her face,
Ella surrendered, that ended the chase.

The summer passed by with Ella still there.
She was chilled by the first touch of frost in the air.
All the leaves on the trees had turned yellow and brown,
And the brisk autumn breeze sent them fluttering down.
Flocks of wild geese scurried off through the sky
Hurrying southward and Ella knew why.

The winter arrived with a howl and a shriek,
Leaving the countryside snowy and bleak.
And poor Ella's feet and her trunk and her toes
And her big, flappy ears and her tail nearly froze.
The cold didn't bother the farmer at all
With his boots and fur cap and his wife's woolen shawl.
And whenever he needed more wood for his stove,
He drove Ella out to the hickory grove.
"It's no use," she said as she trudged through the snow.
"I can never last out the winter, I know."

But somehow poor Ella survived until spring
And this was indeed a most fortunate thing,
For one morning in May (it was barely daylight)
She heard a train toot, and she squealed in delight.
It's the circus train tooting, it's come back today.
No other train whistles exactly that way.
Now I've got to act quickly before Mr. Kirk
Comes out to the barnyard to put me to work.

"I'm sure to end up with a headache," she said
As she backed up a step and then lowered her head.
With a lunge she smashed into the barn door so hard
That the pieces went flying all over the yard.
When old Mr. Kirk heard the earthshaking "boom!"

He had just finished dressing upstairs in his room.
He ran to the window as quick as he could
In time to see Ella dash off toward the wood.
He reached for his shotgun, then called his old hound
And the dog hurried off with his nose to the ground.

They'd have surely caught up to poor Ella with ease
As she blundered along through the dense growth of trees
But the hound had decided to let her go free.
She had suffered enough now for all he could see.
So he led Mr. Kirk on a merry goose chase
Through a dark, soupy swamp and all over the place,
While Ella kept running without looking back
Straight ahead through the forest and on to the track.

And when Ella finally reached the big top,
The whole circus suddenly came to a stop.
The clowns and performers ran out from the tent
And left the crowd wondering where they all went.
Since Ella had left, a whole year had slipped past.
It was hard to believe she had come back at last,
For all of her friends in the circus had missed her.
One clown was so happy he ran up and kissed her.

The very next day as they pulled the tents down
And got the show ready to move out of town,
Ella pitched in to help everyone pack.
She hauled trunks in her trunk and a load on her back.
In fact, she was carrying more than her share
Which seemed most amazing to everyone there.
They didn't know all the things she'd been through
That had helped to unspoil her—but you and I do.

	DATE DUE		
OCT 27 '94	APR 11 '96	JAN 29 2000	
FEB 17 '95	JUL 21 '96	OCT 13 2000	
AUG 1 '95	AUG 15 '96		
FEB 29 '96	NOV 6 4 1998		
AUG 13 '96	DEC 23 1998		
AUG 27			
SEP 18 '96	FEB 12 1999		
JUL 9 '97	FEB 27 1999		
NOV 28 '97	NOV 9 1999		